CU00501184

Ashes to Ashes, Crust to Crust

Pat Wilson

A SAMUEL FRENCH ACTING EDITION

FOUNDED 1830

SAMUELFRENCH.COM
SAMUELFRENCH-LONDON.CO.UK

Copyright © 1976, 1994 by Pat Wilson
All Rights Reserved

ASHES TO ASHES, CRUST TO CRUST is fully protected under the copyright laws of the United States of America, the British Commonwealth, including Canada, and all other countries of the Copyright Union. All rights, including professional and amateur stage productions, recitation, lecturing, public reading, motion picture, radio broadcasting, television and the rights of translation into foreign languages are strictly reserved.

ISBN 978-0-87440-954-3

www.SamuelFrench.com
www.SamuelFrench-London.co.uk

FOR PRODUCTION ENQUIRIES

UNITED STATES AND CANADA
Info@SamuelFrench.com
1-866-598-8449

UNITED KINGDOM AND EUROPE
Theatre@SamuelFrench-London.co.uk
020-7255-4302

Each title is subject to availability from Samuel French, depending upon country of performance. Please be aware that *ASHES TO ASHES, CRUST TO CRUST* may not be licensed by Samuel French in your territory. Professional and amateur producers should contact the nearest Samuel French office or licensing partner to verify availability.

CAUTION: Professional and amateur producers are hereby warned that *ASHES TO ASHES, CRUST TO CRUST* is subject to a licensing fee. Publication of this play(s) does not imply availability for performance. Both amateurs and professionals considering a production are strongly advised to apply to Samuel French before starting rehearsals, advertising, or booking a theatre. A licensing fee must be paid whether the title(s) is presented for charity or gain and whether or not admission is charged. Professional/ Stock licensing fees are quoted upon application to Samuel French.

No one shall make any changes in this title(s) for the purpose of production. No part of this book may be reproduced, stored in a retrieval system, or transmitted in any form, by any means, now known or yet to be invented, including mechanical, electronic, photocopying, recording, videotaping, or otherwise, without the prior written permission of the publisher. No one shall upload this title(s), or part of this title(s), to any social media websites.

For all enquiries regarding motion picture, television, and other media rights, please contact Samuel French.

Please refer to page 23 for further copyright information.

CHARACTERS

Mrs. Martha Murgatroyd -- sister of the departed Jacob Starkie.

Mrs. Parker -- a family friend.

Mrs. Ellis -- who caters privately for funerals, weddings, etc.

Mrs. Booth -- an old lady who just enjoys funerals.

Miss Sarah Starkie -- Jacob's other sister.

TIME
Late afternoon, Christmas Eve.

SCENE
The sitting room of a council house in a West Riding council estate.

to O.G.W.

ASHES TO ASHES,
CRUST TO CRUST

(It is late afternoon on Christmas Eve. Outside it is windy and snowy. The room is the same as before, and as the house is a West Riding 'back-to-back' the Front door, back stage L opens directly onto a small yard in which there is the loo and t'coil (coal hole). The stage is very dim and on central table there is a tatty Christmas tree with some rather ancient fairy lights wired up to the central ceiling light (the only light). there is no cloth on the table and behind the tree is a brown mixing bowl and a large brown tea-pot. Furniture as in the other two plays. Door on SR to kitchen.)

(MRS. MURGATROYD is sitting by table hanging the tree with decorations and some shabby tinsel. She is humming "Good King Wenceslas." Enter MRS. PARKER who has some parcels, some mistletoe and a bag of oranges which she places on table front.)

MRS. PARKER. By! It's a wild neet! And them sacks of coil is nobbut slape.

MRS. MURGATROYD. Aye, well sit you down

MRS. PARKER. Ee, aah see you've gettin t'owd tree out again, Martha.

MRS. MURGATROYD. Aye. Aah reckon it will just about see me out.

MRS. PARKER. *(Hesitantly.)* You do think it right to 'ave decorations and Jacob so recently gone?

MRS. MURGATROYD. Why I doan't knaw, there's noan so

mony Christmases left and ony 'ow, 'ee isn't.

MRS. PARKER. Isn't what?

MRS. MURGATROYD. Gone. Not as you rightly say.

MRS. PARKER. Why? Whear is 'e?

MRS. MURGATROYD. He's in t'coil 'oil. We've putten both caskets in t'coil oil and locked t'door.

MRS. PARKER. Oh! So that is why you 'ave all t'coil stacked in t'yard. It is gettin' to be a bit difficult gettin' in, Martha. It's like climbling ower t'tip.

MRS. MURGATROYD. Aye, Aah knaw. But Sarah gets 'ysterical if we bring 'im into t'house.

MRS. PARKER. Martha Murgatroyd, I can't understand why you can't get shot of 'im.

MRS. MURGATROYD. (*Bitterly.*) You try! Just you try to get rid o' a casket full of creemation ashes. You leave it on a bus and t'conductor gallops after you wi' it. You drop it in t'cut and some daft kids hoik it out and you 'ave to give 'em a reward. Leave it on a seat in t'park and t'attendent comes running after you. (*Passionately.*) If 'e were a bomb I could 'ave left 'im on t'Town Hall steps, and no one would have taken a blind bit o' notice!

MRS. PARKER. Ony road, I thought Mrs. Booth was going to scatter 'im along t'edges of t'allotments to fertilise 'er rabbits.

MRS. MURGATROYD. (*Startled.*) Eh?

MRS. PARKER. I mean for t'ashes to fertilise t'ground so as to make t'dandelions grow for t'rabbits, so she'd have a better Christmas dinner.

MRS. MURGATROYD. Nay, she changed her mind. Ony way, I calls that cannibalism. Nay lass, we 'ad 'im in t'tea. Doan't let's have 'im in a rabbit. I doan't want putting off rabbits.

Besides, she's 'aving a goose wi' t'money Jacob left her. And
that reminds me, you 'aven't 'ad your ten pund yet. (*She goes
to sideboard for her purse and gives Mrs. Parker the money.*)

MRS. PARKER. (*Taking money.*) Ee, thank you, lass. Jacob
were a right good soul, that 'ee were.

MRS. MURGATROYD. Aye, I suppose so, but I do wish 'ee'd
'op off. (*Knocking at door. MARTHA opens it to MRS.
BOOTH and MRS. ELLIS.*)

MRS. ELLIS. By gum, Martha, it's gettin' to be a rare old
scramble climbing over those bags of coil. Why doan't you tip
'em in t'coil 'oil?

MRS. MURGATROYD. Because Jacob's in thear. In fact, both
caskets are in thear. I've hoiked 'em round so much trying to
get rid of 'im that Aa've forgotten which is which.

MRS. BOOTH. 'As Mrs. Parker got 'er money?

MRS. PARKER. Yes, and right thankful.

MRS. BOOTH. Well I think the dear departed 'as at last 'ad
'is wishes attended to, so 'ee might move on. What are you
goin' to get wi' it, Mrs. Parker?

MRS. PARKER. Aah's goin' to get a new coat. Aah 'aven't
'ad one for donkey's years.

MRS. BOOTH. Aah was getting a goose for Christmas, but I
doan't need one now. I'll tell you why in a minute. So I sent
my little grandson in Australia a new jumper and a stamp
album and a gun.

MRS. ELLIS. And I got some new cups and saucers for me
caterin' and some good warm bloomers. What's thu goin' to
get, Martha? Thee and Sarah?

MRS. MURGATROYD. Two hundred pounds is too much to
spend. Ten pounds is easy, but two 'undred is overwhelming.

MRS. PARKER. Two hundred pounds! Whear did t'old devil

get that?

MRS. MURGATROYD. That's just it. We doan't know. That's why we dassen't spend it.

MRS. ELLIS. Ee! Do you think 'e robbed a bank?

MRS. BOOTH. Oh, my Gord! I 'ope not! Aah've spent mine. And they say in t'Argus that they keep a check on t'numbers of stolen notes, and they put invisible dye on 'em that comes up on your 'ands weeks afterwards. Oh, why is it that every time I comes to see you and be neighbourly something horrible happens?

MRS. ELLIS. Don't be so daft, Mrs. Booth. Them notes were donkey's years old.

MRS. MURGATROYD.   Onnyhow, some on 'em were sovereigns.

MRS. ELLIS. 'Ow many?

MRS. MURGATROYD. About fifty.

MRS. ELLIS. Now that is illegal! You could go to jail for hoardin' gold. It all 'as to be kept at Fort Knox.

MRS. MURGATROYD. Whear's that?

MRS. ELLIS. It's a big 'ole in the ground in America.

MRS. MURGATROYD. Well Aah'm noan goin' traipsin' to America to put Jacob's sovereigns into a 'ole in t'ground. They can stop whear they are in 'is boot.

MRS. BOOTH. Well Aah'm right pleased wi' my ten pounds, and Aah've brought my Wee jar to thank 'im wi'.

MRS. ELLIS. We've got enough caskets wi' out a 'wee jar'. What dost thu want a wee jar for?

MRS. BOOTH. It's not a wee jar, it's a Ouija. Look, there's a board wi' letter and numbers on, an' you puts it on t'table like this, an' then we want a glass. Gi' us a glass, Martha.

MRS. MURGATROYD. What for? (*Gets one from sideboard.*)

MRS. BOOTH. Now then, we puts t'glass upside down on t'board and we all put a finger on it an' shuts our eyes and ask it things. An' it goes round t'board an' spells out t'answer.

MRS. ELLIS. 'Ow do we know if we've got us eyes shut?

MRS. BOOTH. Well, we opens 'em when it stops travellin'.

MRS. MURGATROYD. Well, we can but try. (*THEY all put their fingers on glass.*)

MRS. BOOTH. Now all we've got to say is 'Jacob, knock three times if you're there.' An' when 'ee does we say, 'Thank you, Jacob, for t'brass. Now go rest in peace.'

MRS. MURGATROYD. An' then what happens?

MRS. BOOTH. Why, then t'ashes will disappear in a puff of smoke, and you can send t'casket to t'jumble sale.

MRS. ELLIS. Well what's t'point of that if 'ee isn't goin' to say owt?

MRS. BOOTH. Well 'ee might.

MRS. ELLIS. Aah think you've got this mixed up wi' a seeance.

MRS. BOOTH. Well it's t'same thing.

MRS. ELLIS. Well it might be worth a try.

MRS. MURGATROYD. Aye, but we mun have Jacob 'ere or it might go wrong. An' then t'Christmas tree or one o' us might go up in a puff o' smoke.

MRS. PARKER. Whear's Sarah, onnyhow?

MRS. MURGATROYD. She's gone out for some of that instant bread mix. If she sees owt on t'telly she allus has to try it. Even aftershave lotion.

MRS. BOOTH. Oh aye, but what's bread mix?

MRS. ELLIS. It's some newfangled doodah. You just puts t'flour as 'as already got salt an' yeast in it into t'bowl, then you puts half a pint o' water into it, stirs it up and it rises and

you pops it into t'oven and Bob's your uncle. T'slogan is
'There's no need to knead."

MRS. BOOTH. Aah like to kneed bread, myself. It's my
system.

MRS. PARKER. What system?

MRS. BOOTH. Why, I likes 'ome made bread, but it gives
me the wind. But kneading bread breaks me wind, so Aah
makes it, bakes it, eats it, an' gets t'wind. Then I kneads some
more and gets t'wind up.

MRS. PARKER. Oh!

MRS. ELLIS. Ah prefers bicarbonate o' soda, but then Aah
nivver make bread.

MRS. BOOTH. Then you should try cinder tea. Stick a red
hot poker in a cup of cold water an' drink t'water while it
fizzes. But talking of cinders, we can't use the wee jar wi' out
Jacob.

MRS. MURGATROYD. I'll go an' get 'im. Aah'm past bein'
scared.

MRS. BOOTH. Aah'll hold t'candle at t'door, otherwise you
might break your neck ower t'sacks o'coil. (*She takes a candle
from sideboard, lights it and goes to door which she opens in
a flurry of wind and snow.*) By, what a neet. It's nearly dark
an' it's nobbut four o'clock. (*Exit Martha.*) Have you got 'im,
Martha? (*Shouting. Martha struggles back and they close the
door with a slam.*)

MRS. MURGATROYD. Aye, 'ah've got 'im.

MRS. BOOTH. Are you sure you've got t'right casket?

MRS. MURGATROYD. Aye, but take t'lid off an' we'll 'ave a
look. (*They remove lid and gather round closely.*) Aye, it's
'im.

MRS. PARKER. Well shove 'im behind t'tree. Ee gives me

the creeps.

MRS. MURGATROYD. Shove t'bread bowl along, and t'tea pot, then you won't see 'im. Now what do we do?

MRS. BOOTH. We all sit down an' put our fingers on t'glass. it's a pity Sarah isn't here.

MRS. BOOTH. I saw this once on t'telly and t'woman went into a trance. I shall see if Aah can. (*In a sepulchral voice.*) Jacob Starkie, Jacob Starkie. Are you there? (*Back to her usual voice.*) You sometimes get a Red Indian.

MRS. ELLIS. (*Startled.*) A what?

MRS. BOOTH. A Red Indian. They seem to like coming ower from t'other side.

MRS. MURGATROYD. Aah'd rather see Jacob than get a Red Indian. What do they eat?

MRS. ELLIS. Curry.

MRS. MURGATROYD. What the heck is that?

MRS. BOOTH. Nivver mind. If 'e does come, 'ee'll go back. 'Ee won't want 'is tea.

MRS. MURGATROYD. If 'ee does 'ee's going to 'ave fatty cakes an' tripe, same as us.

MRS. BOOTH. Nay lass, let's get into t'right frame o'mind. Let's sit quiet and sing a 'ymn.

MRS. ELLIS. What 'ymn.

MRS. PARKER. I only knows 'Good King Wenceslas.'

MRS. BOOTH. That'll do, it's Christmas. Shur your eyes, an' think o' Jacob. (*THEY sit with their fingers on the glass, and sing the first verse of the carol. Enter Sarah with a bag of flour. She is as usual in a wild rush.*)

MISS STARKIE. 'Ello, 'avin' a carol party? 'Ere, let me join in. Aah'll just make t'bread. (*In the dim light she tips the bag of flour onto Jacob's ashes. She gallops into the kitchen and returns with a jug of water which she pours on to the flour. Stirs madly and then sits down.)* There now, Aah'll join in t'second verse. T'lights on t'tree will help t'dough to rise. *(She starts to sing:)* Brightly shone the moon that night, though the frost was cruel . . .

MRS. BOOTH. *(Rising and speaking in a horrified voice.)* Sarah, you'ved mixed Jacob wi' t'dough! An' 'ee's beginnin' to rise already!

MRS. MURGATROYD. Oh Gawd! You said he'd rise in a puff o' smoke, not in a yeasty loaf.

MISS STARKIE. *(Madly.)* Jacob? How did 'ee get in 'ere? What's 'ee doin' in t'bread? Aah shall go mad. Why is Jacob rising wi' t'dough? Put the light on, Martha. An' let's see what's 'appening.

MRS. MURGATROYD. I can't. Aah've got t'tree lights wired up to t'light thing instead o' t'bulb an' Aah can't think whear Aah've put t'bulb.

MISS STARKIE. Well we must 'ave some more bulbs.

MRS. BOOTH. We could'ave done that.

MISS STARKIE. Done what?

MRS. BOOTH. Planted bulbs in 'is ashes. They would'ave been out by Christmas.

MISS STARKIE. *(Confused.)* What are you talking about? What would 'ave been out?

MRS. BOOTH. Crocuses, or daffies. Mind you, I like crocuses. But you can only grow t'purple sort in t'house. White one allus bolts. Still, it's too late now. *(Gets up and looks at casket.)* By gum, 'ee is rising. Ectoplasm, that's what it is.

MRS. PARKER. What the heck is ectoplasm?

MRS. BOOTH. It's when a body materializes. First in a grey

mist, then like putty, and it tacks shape. It will be Jacob materializing. Unless it's t'Red Indian.

MRS. MURGATROYD. (*Getting hysterical.*) Push 'im back into 'is coffin, I mean 'is casket. We doan't want no Red Indians 'ere.

MISS STARKIE. It's no good. It's up to t'top o' t'casket now. Stop it afore it gets into t'room.

MRS. PARKER. (*Goes to table and struggles with dough.*) There, Aah've bunged some of it into t'tea pot.

MISS STARKIE. What for? 'Ee's been in there afore.

MRS. BOOTH. Nay, 'ee wasn't. You only thought 'ee was. Onny'ow, now 'ee's an 'af an' arf. 'Arf in t'tea pot an' arf in t' casket. (*Sarah shrieks.*) Now what's up?

MISS STARKIE. 'Ee's comin' out o' t'spout.

MRS. MURGATROYD. Well let's take 'im into t'shed where 'ee belongs. (*Martha picks up casket and goes towards the door.*)

MISS STARKIE. Oh Gawd! Jacob will be t'death o' me.

MRS. BOOTH. (*Dashing after Martha with tea pot.*) 'Ere, Martha, take t'other half.

MRS. ELLIS. (*Running after them.*) Nay, don't take 'im outside, Martha. You aren't going to solve anything like that. Think of t'coil.

MRS. MURGATROYD. Aye, Aah knows. Aah gets a regular delivery from t'Co-op. Two bags a week, an' it comes, hell or high water. You can't stop Herbert Fitzackerly!

MISS STARKIE. An' it takes some explaining why he can't put it in t'coil oil. An' 'ee wants 'is bags back. (*All return gasping, and sit down, leaving casket and tea pot on table where they were before.*)

MRS. ELLIS. Ee, Sarah. Sit down, you look done in. 'Ave a cup o' tea.

MISS STARKIE. 'Ow can Aah? Wi' Jacob in t'tea pot rising and rising.

MRS. BOOTH. 'Ee seems to 'ave a liking for that tea pot.

MISS STARKIE. (*Shuddering.*) Well he won't much longer. If 'ee swells up much more it'll bust, and then we'll 'ave to scrape 'im off t'ceiling.

MRS. BOOTH. By gum. There must be summat in them ashes to make t'bread rise. They must be like cinder tea.

MISS STARKIE. Aah shall go mad. Aah know Aah shall go mad. Martha, there must be some way o' gettin' rid o' 'im. What do other people do?

MRS. BOOTH. Aah've been findin' out. You take t'ashes to t'Creematorium an' they scatter 'em in t' garden o' remembreance.

MRS. MURGATROYD. Why didn't we do that afore?

MISS STARKIE. Because Jacob wanted to be scattered in t'cricket field.

MRS. ELLIS. Well we can't do that now. It's all roped off for flats.

MRS. MURGATROYD. Well we mun go tomorrow to t'Creematorium an' ask them to do t'scatterin'.

MISS STARKIE. Don't be daft. We can't take t'tea pot full o'dough oozin' out and t'other part of t'body in t'casket boilin' and bubblin' over t'top, and say, "Wilst thu scatter these? They're our Jacob who died ower a month ago." Besides, who is goin' to hoik out lumps o' claggy dough an' try to scatter it? It'll come out in a lump -- two lumps. Save for t'bit as is oozin o' t'spout.

MRS. BOOTH. Why not take it to t'park an' feed it to t'ducks?

MRS. MURGATROYD. Jacob hated ducks. He wouldn't touch

'em. Said there was nowt on t'legs. An' as 'ee never ate a
duck no duck is goin' to eat 'im.

MISS STARKIE. Get away. He never hated ducks. It was
just that 'ee was too mean to buy a duck. We allus 'ad a
frozen chicken at Christmas.

MRS. MURGATROYD. Well ducks is expensive.

MISS STARKIE. Well 'ee 'ad money, 'adn't 'ee?

MRS. MURGATROYD. Aye, but whear did 'ee get it from?
That's what Aah's worried about.

MRS. BOOTH. Well Aah've nivver heard o' onny bank
robberies round these parts.

MRS. MURGATROYD. Well 'ee hardly ever went out. Ee, I do
wish that dough would stop rising.

MISS STARKIE. We've got to do something. Mrs. Ellis, you
think o' things. What shall we do? By mornin' we won't be
able to get out of t'front door if this goes on. It's going to take
a miracle to stop it.

MRS. ELLIS. Nay lass, not a miracle. They don't happen
nowadays. But Aah've got an idea. Is t'oven on?

MISS STARKIE. Aye. I put it on afore I went out. Why?

MRS. ELLIS. Well put t'tea pot and t'casket in t'oven.

MRS. MURGATROYD. Ee no! Aah's not 'avin' i'm creemated
twice.

MRS. ELLIS. Baked, Martha, nor cremated.

MRS. MURGATROYD. Well it's all t'same when our Sarah
bakes owt. Allus comes out as black as me hat.

MRS. ELLIS. Well do as I tells you. Aah's the one as
organizes things around here.

MRS. MURGATROYD. Aye, lass, that's right. Well, if you say
so. (*Sarah and Martha take tea pot and casket to kitchen and
return.*)

MRS. ELLIS. Now then, sit you down all of you. T'bread an' Jacob will nobbut take a few minutes and that'll stop t'dough and Jacob getting out o'hand, as it were.

MRS. PARKER. Like Quattermass.

MRS. BOOTH. Why, was 'ee put into t'oven?

MRS. PARKER. Naw. Into a space ship. An' when they took 'im out 'ee started to grow, an' 'ee grew an' 'ee grew into a shapeless mass, an' 'ee spread all over London.

MRS. BOOTH. By gum. Fancy that. Is 'ee still there?

MRS. PARKER. Nay, it were on t'telly.

MRS. BOOTH. Oh. Aah nivver watches t'telly when they 'ave 'orrors on. I switch it off an' go to Bingo. Aah won a see-through nightie t'other neet.

MISS STARKIE. An' a fat lot o' good that'll do you.

MRS. BOOTH. You nivver know. Might 'ave burglars. Onyway, Aah wear me red flannel nightie ower t'top. Onnyhow, Mrs. Ellis, what's t'plan you've got?

MRS. ELLIS. Why, t'vicarage is only a step up t'street. You take Jacob there.

MISS STARKIE. What? Both bits?

MRS. ELLIS. Of course both bits. You can't take a half a body.

MISS STARKIE. I wish we could put 'im together. I feel like a chap as 'as sawn a woman in 'alf an' forgot 'ow to join 'er up again.

MRS. ELLIS. You go wi' Martha to t'Vicar an' tell 'im all about it, and see what 'ee says.

MRS. MURGATROYD. 'Ee'll say we're mad.

MISS STARKIE. We will be this goes on.

MRS. ELLIS. An' tell 'im about t'brass as well. If it is rightly Jacob's you can keep it with a clear conscience. But if you find out it isn't no one can do owt to Jacob now, 'Im being gone.

MRS. MURGATROYD. (*Firmly.*) Thu's right, Mrs. Ellis. Come on, Sarah. Get a couple o' t'oven cloths, 'ee smells done -- on top, at any rate.

MISS STARKIE. Aah'm done. Think o' Jacob wi' a crusty top!

MRS. BOOTH. Come on now, Aah'll 'elp you on wi' your 'ats and coats. (*Does so.*)

MISS STARKIE. (*Starts to sing tunelessly.*)
JACOB 'EE WERE ALWAYS CRUSTY
HALF-BAKED AN' SOFT IN T'HEAD.
NOW 'EE'S JUST AS 'ALF BAKED AND CRUSTY
DEAD IN A LOAF O' BREAD.

MRS. MURGATROYD. Sarah, stop it. Don't start singing daft songs.

MISS STARKIE. Aah can't 'elp it. When Aah get worked up Aah allus do.

MRS. MURGATROYD. Oh come on an' get Jacob. (*They each put on oven gloves and go to kitchen.*)

MRS. PARKER. Ee, Sarah does get carried away. (*Sarah marches through clutching tea pot, followed by Martha with casket. As they march solemnly out, Sarah sings to the tune 'Coming Through the Rye.'*)

MISS STARKIE.
HALF A BODY IN A CADDY
TRYING TO GET OUT.
HALF A BODY IN A TEA POT
COMING THROUGH THE SPOUT. (*THEY exit, leaving door open.*)

MRS. PARKER. I think that was most uncalled for on Sarah's

part.

MRS. ELLIS. So do I. Now shall we have a drop of instant coffee until they come back wi' t'tea pot?

MRS. BOOTH. Nay, 'ah'm 'aving nowt to do wi' that tea pot. Onnyhow, they'll 'ave to crack it. They'll nivver get 'im out otherwise.

MRS. ELLIS. I'll go an' get three cups. (*Exits to kitchen.*)

MRS. PARKER. Dust thou think Jacob's a barghest?

MRS. BOOTH. Nowt o' t'sort. 'Ee's just tryin' to tell us something.

MRS. PARKER. Well Aah wish he'd get it said. Wi' out all this daft carry on. (*Sound off of children singing carols -- Away in a Manger, on tape.*) It's nice to 'ear bairns singing at Christmas.

MRS. BOOTH. Aye, as long as they don't start in July.

MRS. PARKER. (*Goes to door and calls to children.*) Don't try to climb ower t'coil sacks or you'll break your necks. Sing us another verse and Aah'll gi' you an orange each.

VOICE OFF. We don't know another verse, missus. It's not in t'top twenty.

MRS. PARKER. Oh well, we don't want t'top twenty. 'Ere you are, catch. 'Owe many of you are there?

VOICE OFF. Four. (*SHE throws out three more oranges.*) Thanks, missus. Merry Christmas.

MRS. BOOTH AND MRS. PARKER. Same to you. luv.

MRS. BOOTH. Ee, put t'wood in t'oil. That wind is coming straight off t'moor. (*Enter MRS. ELLIS carrying tray with three cups of coffee on it.*)

MRS. BOOTH. Ee, it'll warm me cockles. You know, there's one nice thing about Jacob and all this carry on.

MRS. PARKER. (*Sipping her coffee.*) What's that?

MRS. BOOTH. 'Ee's given me some friends. You an' Mrs. Ellis, an' Sarah an' Martha. Aah were reet scared when Aah fust came, an' even more so on t'second time. But Aah've taken to droppin' in, and by gum, it do make a difference. Aah used to feel it bein' on me own at Christmas.

MRS. ELLIS. Did you get your Christmas card from your son in Australia, Mrs. booth?

MRS. BOOTH. Aye, Aah did an' all, an' a photo of t'bairn. (*Takes it from her bag and hands it round.*) Look, isn't 'ee a bonny? (*The others make appreciative noises.*) An' Aah got a parcel o' Australian food. Came by air, it did. Must 'ave cost a mint. Aah was goin' to ask you all if you'd come and see t'New Year in wi' me. Dust thu know it seems as 'ow when I 'ad something exciting to write about it made 'im write back. Ee, Jacob's done me a power a good.

MRS. ELLIS. 'Ow nice. Well Aah'll be glad to come.

MRS. PARKER. Me too. By, it's goin' to be a good Christmas. An' us wi' ten pund to spend and now a do for t'New Year. We ought to 'ave a fust footing.

MRS. BOOTH. Nay, we don't know ony men except Jacob, and we 'ope to be shot o' 'im and 'ee restin' in peace by then. (*Mrs. Ellis gathers up the coffee things and takes them off. When she returns they all sit.*) They should be back soon, 'tis nobbut a step.

MRS. PARKER. Aah 'ope t'Vicar treats 'em kindly.

MRS. ELLIS. Oh, 'ee will. 'Ee's one o' t'old sort. Ee mun be getting on for eighty, must t'Vicar.

MRS. BOOTH. Aye, an' them as lives longest sees most. (*There is a crash outside and Martha and Sarah enter in a rush.*)

MRS. MURGATROYD. Nay Sarah, take care.

MISS STARKIE. Dam' t'coil. Aah'm allus barkin' me shins on them sacks. Onnyhow, we can put t'coil back in t'shed. We've 'ad a miracle.

REST. 'Ow, why? What happened?

MISS STARKIE. Well it were like this . . .

MRS. MURGATROYD. We told 'im all about it, an' about t'brass, an' 'ee said . . .

MISS STARKIE. That our Jacob were a 'ero . . .

MRS. MURGATROYD. An' we knew nowt about it.

MISS STARKIE. It were t'pigeons, see.

MRS. BOOTH. Pigeons? What 'ave they got to do wi' it?

MISS STARKIE. (*Waving her arms about madly.*) Because they were up in t'loft. Hundreds of 'em.

MRS. MURGATROYD. Sarah, sit down afore you 'ave one o' your turns.

MISS STARKIE. (*Capsizing.*) All right, you tell 'em.

MRS. MURGATROYD. Well it were like this, see. T'Vicar said, sixty years ago there were a great fire a t'mill, an' Jacob an' all t'other lads were 'elping to put it out.

MISS STARKIE. But t'wind were blowin' an' it were snowing, an' it were Christmas Eve, just t'same.

MRS. MURGATROYD. An' t'fire spread right up t'streat to t'loft whear everyone kept their pigeons.

MRS. BOOTH. That's nowt, they still do.

MRS. MURGATROYD. Aye. Well all t'birds were goin' up to get roasted and everyone were right moithered, but Jacob tied a wet sack around 'is head, climbed up a ladder all among t'flames, and opened t'door, an' all t'birds flew out in a great cloud, circled round an' flew away.

MRS. BOOTH. Nivver! An' were that t'miracle?

MISS STARKIE. Nay. Jacob got all 'is clothes burnt, an' is

'ands. An' it were all written down in t'Pigeon Fanciers Weekly. An' everyone sent 'im money, an' that's whear t'brass came from.

MRS. PARKER. Ee! That were a miracle.

MISS STARKIE. Nay, we 'avent got to it yet.

MRS. MURGATROYD. Onnyhow, t'Vicar took t'casket an' shook t'dough out o' it onto 'is bird table. then 'ee broke t'tea pot an' put t'rest o' Jacob on t'bird table, an' then 'ee blessed it, an' then 'ee said 'Rest in peace, Jacob Starkie,' and then 'ee laughed an' said 'Ashes to ashes, crust to crust,' and then ...

MRS. PARKER. Go on.

MRS. MURGATROYD. (*Dramatically.*) Well in spite of t'wind an' it being dark a great cloud of pigeons swooped down and picked up t'crumbs an' flew away!

MRS. BOOTH. 'Ee! An' what did t'Vicar say?

MRS. MURGATROYD. Aah don't rightly know. 'Ee said summat about another miracle, wi' Jacob an' a ladder.

MRS. BOOTH. Ee by gum! An' then what?

MRS. MURGATROYD. Nowt much. 'Ee said did we want t'casket, an' we said 'Noa,' an' then 'ee said 'Oh well, Aah'll use for me baccy.' Then 'ee wished us a Merry Christmas an' shut the door.

MISS STARKIE. An' it will be a Merry Christmas. Jacob's gone, t'casket's gone, no more 'avin' tea off t'mangle, no more fallin' ower t'coils . . .

MRS. MURGATROYD. An' two 'undred punds to spend, and Jacob safely gone aloft.

MRS. BOOTH. Or into some pigeon loft.

MRS. MURGATROYD. Aye, that's right. Onnyhow, God bless thee, Jacob, wherever thee is.

* * *

GLOSSARY

Allus -- always
Baccy -- tobacco
Bairns -- children
Barghest -- ghost
Bolts -- blooms, then dies quickly
Coil -- coal
Hoiked -- lifted
Neet -- night
Nivver -- never
Nobbut -- nothing but
Onnyhow -- anyhow
Owt -- anything
Slape -- slippery
Summat -- something
T'coil oil -- the coal hole

MUSIC USE NOTE

Licensees are solely responsible for obtaining formal written permission from copyright owners to use copyrighted music in the performance of this play and are strongly cautioned to do so. If no such permission is obtained by the licensee, then the licensee must use only original music that the licensee owns and controls. Licensees are solely responsible and liable for all music clearances and shall indemnify the copyright owners of the play(s) and their licensing agent, Samuel French, against any costs, expenses, losses and liabilities arising from the use of music by licensees. Please contact the appropriate music licensing authority in your territory for the rights to any incidental music.

IMPORTANT BILLING AND CREDIT REQUIREMENTS

If you have obtained performance rights to this title, please refer to your licensing agreement for important billing and credit requirements.